FROG HUNT

For Robert Weisberg.
The King.
Need I say more?

FROG HUNT

by

Sandra Jordan

ROARING BROOK PRESS

Brookfield, Connecticut

On a bright
summer morning
we set out
to catch a frog.

We see tadpoles,
plump and lazy
on the pond bottom.
Someday
they will grow
into frogs.

A skimmer darts and hovers.

A muskrat waddles past in the shallow water,

then paddles beside us
using her long tail for a rudder.

We know frogs are hiding
in the grassy green reeds,
but we can't find one.

A school of minnows silvers the water.

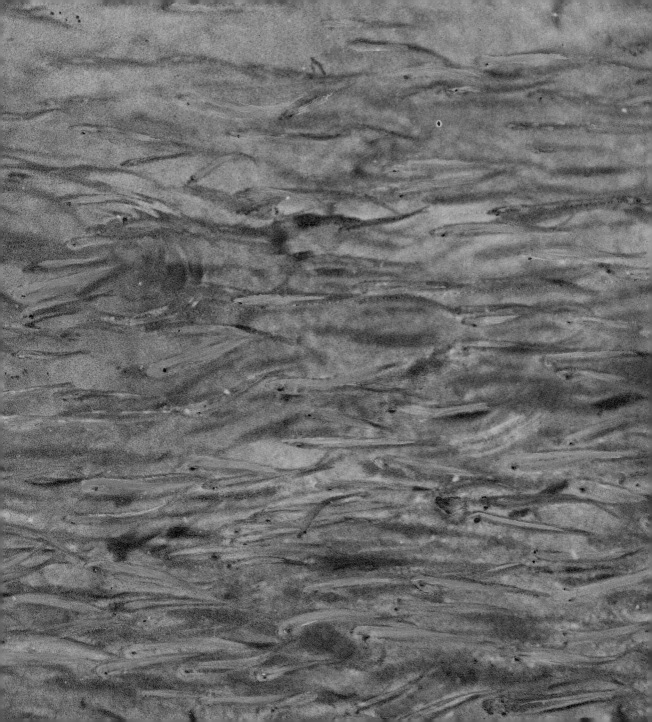

We see a toad on a sandy bank;

then he hops away.

All day long
we look and look.
We hear frogs'
croaking voices.
Where can
they be?

Water lilies
bloom.

A painted
turtle suns
herself on the
willow roots.

We watch a fish
swim back and forth,
back and forth.

The day is ending.
We are ready to go
home. And then
we see a golden eye
gleaming in the reeds.

Got him!
We take turns holding our frog,
feeling the heartbeat through
his thin, cool skin.

Then we
let him go

and watch him swim away.

Thank you frog.
Goodbye.
Tonight, while we
sleep, you'll croak
your froggy song
to the moon and
the trees and the
dark pond water.
But we'll be back
to look
for you again
on a
summer morning.

ABOUT THE POND

Glaciers, thick sheets of ice, once covered part of North America. As the climate changed they slowly melted and retreated north. Chunks of ice as big as buildings broke off and were left behind. Eventually, the chunks also melted, leaving depressions in the earth that filled with water to become ponds. The ponds, called kettle ponds, are a beautiful yet fragile environment. Our family has a one-minute pond rule—if you catch something, return it where you found it within a minute. No creatures leave the pond. (Page 27) Frogs are amphibians. Their eggs hatch into tadpoles who live entirely in the water. The tadpoles grow legs and change into frogs who can live in or out of the water. If you net a tadpole quickly place it in a bucket of pond water while you observe it. (Page 6) The muskrat lives beside the pond. She has partially webbed back feet which make her a good swimmer. Do not get too close. Her teeth are sharp. (Page 9) Toads and frogs are members of the same family. This toad has dry warty skin and short legs. (Page 16) The frog has smooth skin and long legs. (Page 26) The male fish clears the weeds from a space on the pond floor to make a nest. Then he waits for the female to lay eggs so he can fertilize them. (Page 22) Frogs are nocturnal, which means they stay up at night. If you live near a pond, on spring and summer evenings you can hear the frogs calling to each other.

I'd like to thank my two chief frog catchers, Michael and Max Weisberg, as well as all the other people who let me take photographs of their pond days—my sister, Nancie Jordan Weisberg, Robert Weisberg, Katie Weisberg, Stephen Seigel, Amy Cabrita, Donna and Bronwyn Roberts and Lisa, Jane, and Daniel Finn-Foley. And thanks also to George Nicholson, my agent, Neal Porter, my editor, and Jennifer Browne, the designer of *Frog Hunt.* What would I do without you guys?

A Neal Porter Book   Copyright © 2002 by Sandra Jordan.   Published by Roaring Brook Press, a division of The Millbrook Press, 2 Old New Milford Road, Brookfield, Connecticut 06804   All rights reserved
Library of Congress Cataloging-in-Publication Data   Jordan, Sandra   Frog Hunt / Sandra Jordan.   p.   cm.
Summary: A group of children set out on a summer morning to catch a frog and along the way they observe a muskrat, minnows, and a fish as well.   ISBN 0-7613-1592-6 (trade)   0-7613-2652-9 (library binding)   [1. Ponds—Fiction.   2. Frogs—Fiction.]
PZ7.j7683 Fr 2002   [E]—dc21   2001041714   Printed in Hong Kong
library: 10   9   8   7   6   5   4   3   2   1   trade: 10   9   8   7   6   5   4   3   2   1